In memory of Margaret Hamilton,
who had a little magic of her own.
~ M.P.H.

Art copyright © 2004 by Leo and Diane Dillon
Text copyright © 1987 Michael Patrick Hearn

Jacket design by Kelly Hitt.

A publication of Milk and Cookies Press, a division of ibooks, inc.

Distributed by Simon & Schuster, Inc.
1230 Avenue of the Americas, New York, NY 10020

This book is a work of fiction.
Any resemblance to actual events or locales or persons, living or dead, is entirely coincidental.

ibooks, inc.
24 West 25th Street, 11th floor, New York, NY 10010

The ibooks, inc. World Wide Web Site address is:
http://www.ibooks.net

ISBN 0-689-03592-6
First ibooks, inc. printing: September 2004
10 9 8 7 6 5 4 3 2 1

Editor – Dinah Dunn

Library of Congress Cataloging-in-Publication Data available

Manufactured in China

THE PORCELAIN CAT

BY MICHAEL PATRICK HEARN
ILLUSTRATED BY LEO AND DIANE DILLON

MILK &
COOKIES
PRESS

NEW YORK
DISTRIBUTED BY SIMON & SCHUSTER, INC.

Late one evening, when the candles had burned down to stubs, the Sorcerer sat staring into an ancient book. While studying a rare Peruvian charm for turning toads into hummingbirds, he heard something dart in and out of the cupboards. "Rats!" he said, and turning back to his book, he found that half a page had been gnawed away by the vermin.

"I must do something about these pests!" he mumbled. Scanning the room, full of bottles and books, his eye fell on a porcelain cat. It had been a gift from his aunt, a witch of great abilities but little taste. He had never cared for it, and now it stood stiffly as a paperweight. "Ah, that is it," he declared. "I shall bring the cat to life and set it on the rats. It is about time I found some use for it."

The Sorcerer sorted through a shelf of books and pulled out a heavy volume bound in leopard skin. On finding a spell for bringing china to life, he cried, "Ah, ha! This is just what I need." The charm was simple enough, but it called for a vial of basilisk blood, and there was none in the cupboard.

The Sorcerer grabbed his sleeping apprentice by his dirty collar and shook him from his dreams. "Nickon! Nickon!" he cried. "You must go find a vial of basilisk blood for me *this very instant!*"

The drowsy boy wanted to say something about how vile he thought the request was, but instead he only grumbled, "And where am I to find it at this hour?"

"You must go to the Witch Beneath the Hill, of course," the old man said. "She never sleeps, and she owes me a favor. So be gone before I box your ears!"

The night was chilly, so Nickon went quickly. As he had gone with his master many times to the witch's hut, he knew the way through the tangled wood. Within minutes he stood before her door, at the base of a grassy mound that rose from the middle of the forest. He rapped loudly on the door, and the old witch shouted for him to enter. He knew at once she was not in the best of humors. She was clumsily bandaging a hand that apparently she had just burned. "What do you want?" she snapped.

"My master has sent me for a vial of basilisk blood," began the boy. "He says that you owe him a favor and that you must give it to me immediately."

"Owe him a favor? Nonsense!" she cried. "He gave me a powder he said would cure warts. Cure warts! It could not cure a headache! I owe him nothing. But, if you wish to please your master, you must please me first!"

"And how can I do that?" asked the troubled apprentice.

"There is a salve made from a certain shellfish that can cure any burn," she explained. "Go get some of that shellfish from the Undine of the Brook, and I will give you what you wish."

Nickon agreed and once again set out through the night. The moon was full and ripe, and the boy soon came to a forest brook, bordered by a field of rushes. He had read somewhere that water maidens dwell at the mouth of rivers, so he followed the stream to its source.

"Undine, Undine," he called to the water. "Come to me. I must ask a favor."

The clear water rushed from smooth stones and pink shells dotting the river's mouth; and soon a water maiden raised her lovely head. "Yes, yes," she spoke, in a whisper that would have silenced a storm at sea. "What is it you wish, my boy?"

"The Witch Beneath the Hill has injured her hand and must have the shellfish whose salve can cure any burn."

The maiden laughed. "To receive your shellfish, you must do something for me." She dove beneath the water and reappeared with a basket woven of the river reeds. "Gather me a basketful of the red-spotted mushrooms that grow in the wood," she whispered.

"They are delicious, but alas, they do not grow by the banks of my river. Hurry, for they vanish at the coming of morning. And then you shall have your shellfish." She threw him the basket and slipped beneath the water.

Nickon picked up the basket and stumbled on through the underbrush as the forest grew wilder. He found nothing until he came upon a small clearing. In a ring of moonlight grew a circle of the red-spotted mushrooms. He quickly gathered them up, but when he bent to pluck the last one, he was stopped by the tip of an arrow.

"How dare you pick my mushrooms?" demanded a gruff voice.

The boy looked up and trembled, for before him stood a strange creature, half man and half horse. It was the dreaded Centaur of the Wood. "Please, please," Nickon pleaded, nearly in tears. "I must have them. I have to give them to the Undine of the Brook, so she will give me shellfish, so I can give those to the Witch Beneath the Hill, so she will give me a vial of basilisk blood for which my master, the Sorcerer, has sent me!"

"Ah, you foolish, faithful servant," said the man-beast with a rumbling laugh. "As you are so ready to do favors, I too have one to ask of you. I am cloven-hooved and cannot climb the tangled trees. If you will climb one and throw down the ripe fruit to me, you may have the mushrooms."

This did not seem like much to ask to save his life, so the boy agreed, and he climbed up the tallest tree and threw the fresh, ripe fruit down to the centaur, who greedily gathered it up in a leather pouch.

"A bargain is a bargain," said the centaur, as he handed the basket of mushrooms to the boy. "Jump on my back, and I will take you to the brook."

Nickon dropped down on the back of the man-beast, and the centaur galloped

through the thick wood so swiftly that the night whistled in their ears. When they arrived at the reedy bank by the mouth of the brook, the boy jumped from the creature's back and gratefully said good-bye.

"Undine, Undine!"
Nickon called to the
stream. "Come to me,
please, come to me!"

The lovely head once more rose from the water, and the Undine's green eyes glittered at the sight of the precious mushrooms.

"Please give me the shell-fish as you promised," Nickon spoke. "Those that can cure any burn."

"Oh, yes, a bargain is a bargain," she replied, as she slid beneath the water. In less than a moment she returned and held aloft a handful of the pink shellfish. "Put them safely in the basket, and you must have a boat!"

As she spoke, a small but sturdy vessel woven of river reeds appeared at the brook's mouth. It was just large enough to hold the boy, and the water maiden whispered, "Hurry, get in, get in! I will take you to the Witch Beneath the Hill!" Then, without a word, she swiftly drew the little boat down the stream to where the witch lived.

"I must leave you now," said the Undine, and she disappeared beneath the water. The boy leaped from the boat to the bank, and as he did, the boat fell apart, leaving the reeds to float away with the brook.

Nickon ran to the witch's door. Her lamp was out, as it was nearly dawn, but he rapped as loudly as he could. The witch shouted several ugly curses, but she opened the door, crying, "What do you want now?"

"I have the shellfish," Nickon proclaimed, "and now I must have the vial of basilisk blood!"

"Go away," she grumbled. "After you left, I remembered I still had some dried shellfish in the root cellar. Go away! I do not need any more."

"But a bargain is a bargain!" cried the desperate boy.

"Oh, so it is," she admitted reluctantly as she went to her cupboard. "Here is what you want. Give me the shellfish—I will find some use for them."

Relieved that he had finally secured what his master demanded, Nickon quickly made the exchange and ran off into the morning light.

The Sorcerer had not moved a muscle since the boy's departure, but at Nickon's triumphant arrival, the old man jumped three times on his left foot—he was that delighted. He took the vial of the precious blood and gathered up the other ingredients for the charm. He then mixed and stirred and chanted over the bubbling pot, and soon all was done. The brew had boiled down to a thin gray liquid.

When it was ready, the Sorcerer filled a tin cup with the precious mess and poured it all over the porcelain cat, which still sat stiffly as a paperweight. He chanted something that made no sense and watched the strange workings of his charm.

The glass eyes of the cat flamed, and as it stiffly moved its head back and forth on its thick neck, a rat scurried out of the darkness. Instantly the cat leaped into the air after it and landed hard on the

stone floor, shattering into a thousand pieces.

"Nickon, clean up this mess!" the Sorcerer shouted. "I never liked that porcelain cat anyway!"

And he went back to his books and left the rats to their business.